Imagine That!

Look for these
Road to Writing
books

Mile 4 • First Journals

The Great Outdoors
Me, Myself, and I

Mile 5 • Journals

Best Friends
Imagine That!

In This Book You Can:

- Make up your own stories.

- Rewrite your stories from other points of view.

- Brainstorm silly topics.

- Be creative!

A GOLDEN BOOK · **New York**
Golden Books Publishing Company, Inc. New York, New York 10106

ISBN: 0-307-45500-9   A MM

Imagine That!

by Sarah Albee
illustrated by Jeff Shelly

BRAINSTORM!

Things I want to learn to do:

1. _____

2. _____

3. _____

4. _____

5. _____

This will be fun!

Pick one.
Why do you want
to learn it?

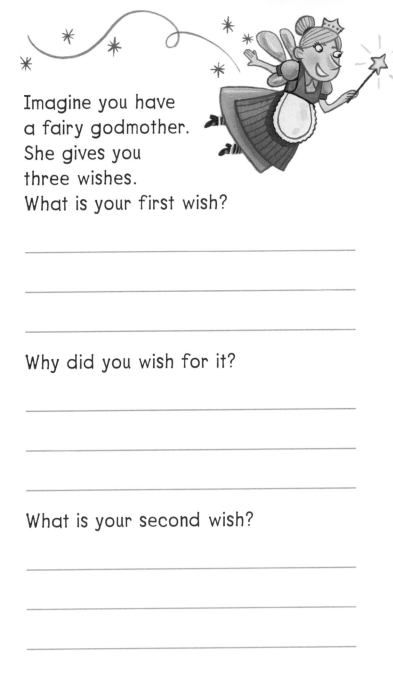

Imagine you have
a fairy godmother.
She gives you
three wishes.
What is your first wish?

_____

_____

_____

Why did you wish for it?

_____

_____

_____

What is your second wish?

_____

_____

_____

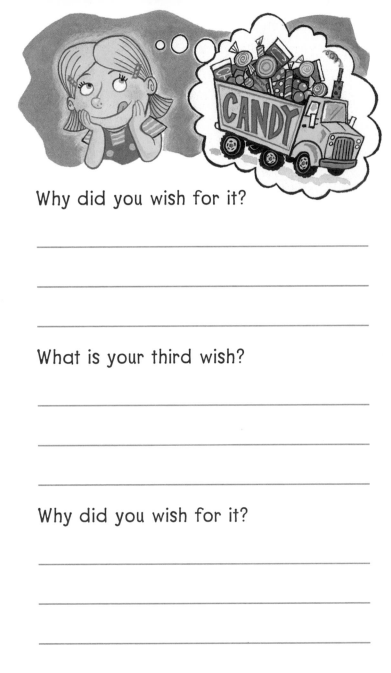

Why did you wish for it?

_____

_____

_____

What is your third wish?

_____

_____

_____

Why did you wish for it?

_____

_____

_____

Imagine you're a secret agent.
Create a secret language.
Invent meanings for these words.

snerge (noun): _____

bambut (verb): _____

retasment (noun): _____

floop (verb): _____

Invent words for these meanings.

_____ (noun)

a getaway car

_____ (verb)

to go on a wild goose chase

_____ (noun)

a hidden staircase

_____ (verb)

to stumble on a clue

Make up your own words and meanings.

_____

_____

_____

_____

_____

Imagine you have
a superhuman power.
What is it?
Write about it.

_____

_____

_____

_____

_____

_____

_____

_____

_____

_____

On second thought…
read what you wrote
on the last page.
Is there anything
you want to change?
Write it over with your changes.

_____

_____

_____

_____

_____

_____

_____

_____

_____

If you could pick
the perfect job,
what would it be?

Describe a day at work.

_____

_____

_____

_____

_____

_____

_____

_____

_____

_____

_____

Things I'm not allowed to do
(but wish I could):

1. _____

2. _____

3. _____

4. _____

5. _____

Pick one.
Write about why
you want to do it.

_____

_____

_____

_____

_____

_____

_____

_____

_____

Imagine you can fly.
Where will you go?

_____

_____

_____

_____

_____

_____

_____

_____

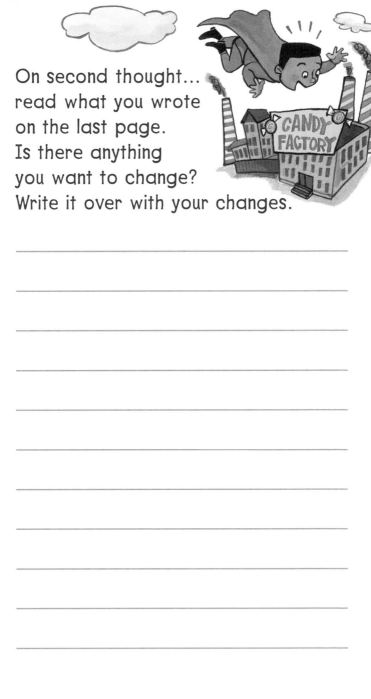

On second thought...
read what you wrote
on the last page.
Is there anything
you want to change?
Write it over with your changes.

_____

_____

_____

_____

_____

_____

_____

_____

_____

Your brain tells the rest
of your body how to
ride a bike.
Write out all the directions.

Feet:

_____

_____

_____

_____

Eyes:

_____

_____

_____

_____

_____

Hands:

_____

_____

_____

_____

_____

Legs:

_____

_____

_____

_____

_____

If you could be one age for the rest
of your life, what age would you
choose?
Why?

_____

_____

_____

_____

_____

_____

_____

_____

_____

_____

ALIEN LANDS ON EARTH!

You're a reporter.
Write a story that goes with this picture.

_____

_____

_____

_____

_____

_____

_____

_____

_____

_____

Your friend invites you to
visit his planet.
But they only eat meatloaf.
Make up five polite reasons
why you can't go.

1. _____

2. _____

3. _____

4. _____

5. _____

Pick an excuse.
Write a letter to your friend.

Date_____

Dear_____,

_____

_____

_____

_____

_____

_____

_____

Sincerely,

_____

Imagine you have a potion
that makes people tell
ONLY the truth.

I would give the potion to:

_____

What questions would you
ask that person?

_____

_____

_____

_____

_____

_____

What do you think the answers
would be?

_____

_____

_____

_____

_____

_____

_____

Safety Tips

1. Never leave a banana peel where your teacher might step on it.

2. Never wake a sleeping bear.

   (Create your own safety tips.)

3. _____

   _____

   _____

   _____

   _____

4. _____

   _____

   _____

   _____

   _____

Pick one of the tips.
Write about what happens if you
don't follow it.

_____

_____

_____

_____

_____

_____

_____

_____

_____

_____

Imagine you could
be any animal.
What would you be?
What would you do?

_____

_____

_____

_____

_____

_____

_____

_____

_____

_____

_____

On second thought...
read what you wrote
on the last page.
Is there anything you
want to change?
Write it over with your
changes.

Much better!

_____

_____

_____

_____

_____

_____

_____

_____

_____

BRAINSTORM!

Reasons why you didn't
do your homework:

1._____

2._____

3._____

4._____

5._____

Pick one.
Write a note to your teacher
using this excuse.

If you could have only one food for a
week, what would you choose?
Why?

_____

_____

_____

_____

_____

_____

Create a recipe using this food.

Hot dog casserole or hot dog pie?

RECIPE

Imagine you are a dolphin.
Write about your day.

First, I woke up.

Next, I went to _____

_____

_____

_____

_____

_____

_____

We believe they can actually talk with one another.

And then I went to sleep.

BRAINSTORM!

Excuses for missing tea with the Queen:

1. _____

2. _____

3. _____

4. _____

5. _____

Pick one.
Write a note to the Queen using
this excuse.

If you could zap yourself into any TV show, which one would you choose?

Why?

Imagine you have the chance to meet your favorite superhero. What will you say?

_____

_____

_____

_____

_____

_____

_____

_____

What will you do?

_____

_____

_____

_____

_____

_____

_____

_____

_____

_____

_____

Imagine Robin Hood wants you to join his band of Merry Men.

What special talent do you have to offer them?

_____

_____

_____

_____

_____

_____

_____

_____

_____

_____

_____

_____

You just won the lottery.
Write what you plan to
do now that you are rich.

_____

_____

_____

_____

_____

_____

_____

_____

_____

_____

On second thought...
read what you wrote
on the last page.
Is there anything you
want to change?
Write it over with your changes.

_____

_____

_____

_____

_____

_____

_____

_____

_____

You're at pirate camp.
Write a letter home.

WALK the PLANK

Date_____

Dear_____,

_____

_____

_____

_____

_____

Love,

_____

BRAINSTORM!

Things you can make with mud:

1. _____

2. _____

3. _____

4. _____

5. _____

Pick one.
Write instructions on how to make it.

_____

_____

_____

_____

_____

_____

_____

_____

_____

_____

_____

If you could be invisible,
where would you go?
What would you do?

_____

_____

_____

_____

_____

_____

_____

_____

_____

_____

_____

Imagine you have become
a famous writer.
Practice your autograph here.

_____

_____

_____

_____